Dementia Diaries

Mitch Levenberg

Also by Mitch Levenberg

Principles of Uncertainty and Other Constants

Write Something

Dementia Diaries

Mitch Levenberg

Irene Weinberger Books/Hamilton Stone Editions
Maplewood, New Jersey

Library of Congress Cataloging-in-Publication Data

Levenberg, Mitch, 1952-
Dementia diaries / by Mitch Levenberg.
  pages ; cm
  ISBN 978-0-9903767-1-2 (acid-free paper)
  1. Mothers and sons--Fiction. 2. Parent and adult
child--Fiction. 3. Dementia--Patients--Care--Fiction. 4.
Diaries--Fiction. 5. Domestic fiction. I. Title.
  PS3612.E92336D46 2015
  813'.6--dc23
                                        2015017960

Printed in the United States of America
First Paper Printing 2015

Irene Weinberger Books/Hamilton Stone Editions
P.O. Box 43, Maplewood, NJ 07040
Ireneweinbergerbooks.com

Dedication

I would like to dedicate the book to my mother and all those who made her life easier during her last five months—Joanie and Cliff, Christine and Garth, and Eli.

I'd also like to thank my daughter Anna Rose Levenberg for all the hard work and time she put in designing the cover.

The Dementia Diaries

Mitch Levenberg

Preface

My mother's birthday dinner at *Giando on the Water* in Williamsburg, Brooklyn would be a small gathering of friends and relatives including George Clooney, that is a poster of George Clooney. The Japanese tourists-who were real-came later, snapping pictures before they found their tables. They were happy and mistook us (or did they) for a tourist attraction. My mother loved it. Ninety, she kept saying. Ninety. I can't believe that number she kept repeating so we purposely didn't put it on the cake. One elderly Japanese gentleman knew though because my sister-in-law speaks Japanese and probably told him because there seemed to be a fresh commotion—a ripple of excitement among their tables. My mother liked this. The old man came over, kissed her on the cheek and then took her picture. Could she have found love again so suddenly with a Japanese tourist at Giando on the Water? Not exactly, since his wife was there too and the both of them soon stood side by side inviting my mother to stay with them in Japan. Within days no doubt, Japan would know all about this—that is about my mother turning 90.

My mother loves attention and on this night, she got it. I felt bad at first I couldn't afford to make her one of those big birthday bashes like some of her relatives or friends' children might—you know inviting 300 of her closest friends, rent out the whole restaurant, or a cruise ship on the Hudson, the Danube, or the intercoastal down in Florida.

I felt out of it. It was really my cousin Marilyn and our very close friend Joanie who found the place and planned it all and even helped pay for it. Then my cousin asked people to chip in on a gift, even me, so where was my gift? Chipping in? Showing up? Was that enough? Where was I in all this, her own son? What could I give my mother that no one else could and without having to spend a lot of money?

Then my wife told me I should write a poem for my mother and read it at the restaurant. I still didn't feel that writing a poem would make up for not paying for all this and more, but I decided to write one anyway. And when the night arrived, sometime after my second or third drink, I read it to her, and everyone else, at the table:

She couldn't
Be 90

I mean
Isn't
That

Too

Old

To still
Look
Like
Marilyn Monroe?

She
Doesn't
Look Ninety
Maybe Sixty

Still floats
Like a butterfly
Stings like a bee

And
If she falls
She gets up
Like Muhammed Ali
(Who by the way
Is only Seventy)

She doesn't
Need
Assisted Living

Or

Home care
She says
Let them put
On their own
Underwear

She loves
To watch
Piers Morgan
And Bill Maher

But most of all
On her refrigerator
Door
For all of Coconut Creek
To see

Is a picture
Of her boyfriend
George Clooney

So
She can't be ninety

Can she?
Her face is so smooth

She's really very
Clever
You can never pull
A fast one on her
Ever

So Laura
Tonight
We

Pour a
Glass for

You
With
All our love
And
Appreciation

Screw the
Medication
Spill it all
Down
The sink
And let's just
Drink drink drink
To you

If we searched
The whole world
Through
And found all kinds

Of others
We'd never
Find

Another Mother
Or Aunt or Grandma

Like you.

My mother loved it. She thanked me. Despite all the times I mentioned she was ninety, she still thanked me. "That was lovely," she said. "Thank you. That was really lovely."

I never really remembered my mother thanking me for much of anything. I mean I never thanked her for very much either. We just weren't a family who thanked each other for much. We never told each other that we loved each other either. These things were just too hard to say, to do. Spending money was much easier— theoretically, of course.

So when my mother thanked me for the poem I felt she had given me a gift as well. She said that she would put it on her refrigerator in Florida next to George Clooney—and that was good enough for me.

The night was a success. Everyone had a good time. My mother was beaming. When she walked out of the restaurant she really did look like Marilyn Monroe during a movie premier, basking in the present—uncertain of the future—and when she was whisked away in someone's car—clutching her rolled up poster of George Clooney—we paparazzi still taking pictures—I suddenly felt very wealthy and hoped more than anything my mother would always remember this night—the night she turned ninety and took George Clooney home.

The Dementia Diaries

"All People with Dementia are Demented in their Own Way"

What do you do when it was your mother you always spoke to about other people and somehow with all her prejudices and skewered ideas about people seemed to be nevertheless right on the mark about them and now that she has become frightened and bitter about these last years or months or days of her life there is nothing much to say or listen to that I know may or may not be true and how now I talk not about other people with my mother but about my mother with other people. I don't like talking to my mother anymore. It makes me sad to feel this way. It frightens me too because when I talk to my mother now it is like talking to an exaggerated more agitated and more nervous and more out of control mother than I have ever known.

Now she has left her home of thirty years and is in an Independent Living Facility. Let's say Residence. Let's say Retirement Home. Whatever it is, she is not happy. In fact, she is very unhappy. She is sure to tell me this every day I speak to her. The place is fine, she says. It's not the place, she says. It's me, she says, and no one can tell me I should be happy when I'm not happy.

The place I guess, if you really think about it, is really more like a hotel. There's a cultural center and fitness center and an arts and crafts studio and an outdoor swimming pool and whirlpool spa and library and beauty salon and movie theater and scheduled and private transportation and three meals a day in a spacious dining room and yet my mother still feels like a prisoner and like a prisoner dreams of escaping one day. I see her one day donning an old raincoat and sunglasses, maybe a mustache for good measure, skulking through the lobby getting into a private cab and heading back to her house which is no longer her house and for which she no longer has the key. Excuse the pun but that's the key—no key.

My mother is depressed. She stopped taking her medication. She stopped taking showers. She stopped going to the beauty salon. She won't go in the pool, or the library, or on a bus to the supermarket or do any arts and crafts or even eat dinner. She hates her best friend who lives there and whose idea it was to live there and who gave my mother the idea and impetus to move there. Now she swears she will never speak to her again. Her friend, Charlotte, is too slow. She doesn't want to do anything except eat, play Bingo, take naps, and smoke cigarettes on the terrace of her room. My mother calls her a deadhead, a loser. The other night—and this was the final straw—my mother waited a half hour for her friend to come down to the dining room where they usually sit together and when Charlotte finally came down she went to sit with two other people instead of my mother and sat at a different table. My mother was highly insulted. She called her far worse things than loser or deadhead. The next day, Charlotte denied the whole thing. That's the thing about having Dementia. Charlotte has even more Dementia than my mother has. I don't have the exact measurements for either of them—besides, as Tolstoy might say, all people with Dementia are demented in their own way—but I know they both forget not just the small things but big things too. Whole days even. They lose track of time. They forget having spoken to someone or someone having visited and they will remember people who were never there at all. So Charlotte had no recollection of having gone off with two people to another table and thus abandoning my mother. My mother didn't care whether she remembered or not. Dementia was no excuse because my mother, even in her own Dementia, finds being slighted and insulted unforgiveable no matter what your excuse is. Besides if they both have Dementia then they're even; their playing field is equal and if my mother feels slighted and insulted than Charlotte should feel she has slighted and insulted her. My mother still has her dignity. This to her is as clear as day. Yes, she is still a lady. How dare anyone imply otherwise—like the home care people I have suddenly thrust upon her—for her own good of course—who throw her into cold showers or make her take her pills or clean up after her. How dare they.

"Dementia vs. Dementia"

My mother went to the beauty parlor every Friday for 60 years and now doesn't seem to care anymore. That's disturbing. It's like when my father didn't feel like reading any more. Big changes.

For both Charlotte and my mother, these are the early stages of Dementia—although as Yogi Berra once said, "It sure gets late early around here," and now it is Dementia vs. Dementia and who will be, not necessarily the last one standing, but perhaps the last one remembering. So, despite everything, of course, they're talking again. What they say to each other, however, no one really knows—most likely not even them—but what difference does it make?

They're medicating my mother now. Making sure she takes her pills. Last time I spoke to her, she sounded heavily medicated. On drugs, you might say. She said she was tired. She said she had done a lot but couldn't remember what she did. It's the nurses she remembers. There are four of them. They're there around the clock. They seem to have become my mother's life. I think she likes having them there. It gives her purpose. It's company. It may be bad company but it's company. Still, she'd rather not have them there. They're in her face. They're up her ass. Sometimes literally. She'd rather not have them there. When I mention that maybe we can cut down on their visits, she says things like "that would be nice," or "if you could I'd really appreciate it." It was satisfying on one hand and scary on the other. This was not the drug free angry mother I knew. To tell you the truth I prefer the drugged one. One thing I always try to do is change my mother and now I see that drugs can do that for me. If I tell her she needs to do something like take her medication or take general care of herself, that we have hired people to help her do that, she gets angry and wants to die anyway although I think she really wants to live more than anything, but just not as a very old person without a husband or boyfriend whose friends and relatives have pretty much all died. When I insist she accept this help she yells, "Why are you doing this to me? Why are you doing this to your mother? Why are you killing your own mother? Why Why Why?" and she reminds me of the "Exorcist" when the devil takes over the priest's mother while she's lying in bed in the nursing home: "Demi, why do you do this to me? Why do you do this to me?" and he yells back, "You are not my mother!" but he is wrong. She is his mother. They are all our mothers. And we are all their sons.

When my own mother yells at me there is something so raw as if she were this 91 year old wound suddenly exposed and everyone she has been angry at consciously or unconsciously over these many years, her own mother and brothers and husband and sons and my own wife who would not let her consume me, suck the life out of me as she did my own brother, was included in that primal scream.

She was angry again last night. "The nurses came too early," she says. "They give me a shower and it's humiliating. They pound me with drugs several times a day." When I ask if she's met any men yet, she says she had a long conversation with a man at breakfast but when she tried to continue it during lunch he had no recollection of ever having spoken to her. I wonder if she ever spoke to him at all or whether she started speaking to the wrong man at lunch or whether, to be fair, he really did forget he had spoken to her. Who knows? But I do tell her that she could have always started a new conversation or the same one over again. Maybe that's a plus about Dementia. You never run out of things to say because you can always have the same conversation over and over again since no one remembers ever having it in the first place. Yes, it's always Ground Hog Day at The Reserve.

My brother e-mails me: "Wow. Just spoke to mother. Wow she is miserable. Never heard her talk this way. Do not want to go into it. Too depressing." Too depressing for him? Just wait. But he knows this. He says the least we should do is change her room but I tell him we can't change her room until another one becomes available. It sounds cold and almost dismissive when I say it like reason or logic have no place here. Then my brother writes back: "Hope the situation gets better down there or things are going to explode." That's actually very perceptive of him, I think.

"You Are the Only Friend I Have"

The next time I talk to my mother she tells me they come every morning at 7 A.M. to her cold room and throw her into a cold shower. When I tell her I doubt the room or the shower is cold she asks me if I'm trying to be funny. I have forgotten she has lost her sense of humor. She also tells me I never believe what she says anymore and though that's not entirely true it's gotten a lot more difficult to and now I really need to check out her facts with other people, most of them complete strangers. When she complains so bitterly about her new life, I tell her she makes me feel like a villain whose put her into prison. I tell her over and over again this is independent living. You can make of it what you will. You can be positive or negative. Obviously, she's chosen to be negative. It is not a nursing home or a torture chamber or a psychiatric hospital, I tell her. You were alone in your house surrounded by young couples and houses that were being robbed and you had no friends because all your friends were dead and no matter how much of a mistake you think it was no matter how bitter you are about leaving your home, you could no longer live there by yourself. And you're just making me feel bad like I'm doing something wrong when all I'm trying to do is the best that I can do for you. I don't even like speaking to you because all you do is cry and complain. "No, no," she says. "You are my only friend. You are the only friend I have. Do you understand that, Mitchell?" she says. "I don't want you to think that way because you are the only friend I have." And when we hang up, I think to myself, how did it ever come to this?

Tonight, my mother has just come back from her apartment from dinner. She says, "I know you don't like to hear me complain." "That's right," I tell her. "I don't." "But the elevator is terrible," she tells me. "It always goes past my floor." That's OK, I think. If it's only the elevator she's complaining about then that's progress. She was waiting for Charlotte again. "Everyone thinks I'm crazy," she says. She comes late all the time. We're the last ones in and the last ones out."

"Getting Too Late For Early Dementia"

Today my mother hates Charlotte again. "She never even asks if I want to come with her to the doctor," she complains. "Although I don't know why I'd want to come to the doctor with her. But sometimes her mother (she means her daughter) takes her to the supermarket after that. Oh, what's the use of talking," she says.

My brother has been talking to my cousin Kenny. Kenny told him that my mother sounds like she's in the early stages of Dementia. He knows that from his wife Marcia who has subsequently passed away. When my brother tells me this, when he says he actually agrees with Kenny that she must indeed be in the early stages of Dementia, that that must be why she seems so confused all the time, you could have knocked me over with a feather. But very early Dementia he is sure to emphasize. Very early? I think to myself. How early does he believe it is? I have very early Dementia. So does he. I can't remember where I put my socks only seconds after I put them somewhere or the name of a young woman I had seen every day at work for months. She worked for me. We talked every day. She tutored my daughter in Math. The other day I saw her pass by my house walking her bike along the street and I wanted to call out her name which I took for granted would fly out of my mouth like it always did but nothing came out because I had forgotten her name completely. But that was very early Dementia because by the time she was half way down the block I remembered part of her name which was close but didn't quite seem right and by the time she was all the way down the block, about to turn the corner, I finally remembered her whole name, so it took a little longer than usual to remember but my mother wouldn't only have forgotten her name but just a few hours later would have forgotten she ever saw her.

In fact, she's really getting mixed up with names. Yesterday, once again, she wasn't speaking to my wife Julie anymore and when she mentioned tables I knew she meant Charlotte again, not Julie—this on—going saga of Charlotte and the two strange ladies and then leaving no room for my mother at the table? What the hell is going on here? And why do nurses keep coming into her room and giving her injections in the leg? Sometimes when I talk to my mother I think she's a character from some absurdist play like Pinter or Pirandello—or maybe Alice in Wonderland. No, it's just getting too late for early Dementia.

"Plants, Books, and a Box of My Uncle's Jokes"

I've been feeling very sad lately. I read a letter recently my father wrote to me in 1996 just before he turned 80. He was looking forward to coming up north to see us again and said that he missed us very much. He said it was much easier to say that in a letter since he wasn't much of a conversationalist. He said he felt like he was 30 except for the arthritis in his knees. He said he was obsessed with two things: Plants and books. He said the other morning he was awoken at 7 A.M. by "the horrible sounds of the bush cutting equipment" mowing the grass and shrubs and what he thought were the flowers— Gardenias and Hibiscus—he planted but when he rolled up the pull ups—much to his relief—they were cutting elsewhere. He said that getting out of bed so quick "can be very detrimental to your health" and that "one should get out of bed very slowly." And now he is gone along with his Gardenias and Hibiscuses. And after he died, whatever grew was destroyed by the cutting machines and no one got up to stop them. I doubt that was because it was detrimental to their health but rather that they just didn't care.

Going through the same box of letters, in which I found my father's, I also found an envelope filled with my uncle Barney's jokes. They just didn't seem funny without him actually telling them. And now he's gone too and so are his jokes which really should have been buried along with him. After all, what was he without his jokes just like what was my father without his books? My father and my uncle—his brother in law— didn't get along very well, but despite it all, I know they enjoyed each other's jokes. Anyhow, that's how I've been thinking about death lately. Who's still here and who isn't here anymore, what they have taken with them and what they have left behind. Things I always enjoyed talking to my mother about.

"I Just Like that Gender"

Tonight my mother seemed in a good mood. She had just gotten back from a show. She had been bored all day and was going to tell me enough is enough and she didn't want to live there anymore. Then she went to this show. Then she spoke to a man from the Bronx. He was very nice, she said. They talked for a long time. I like men," she says. "I like men better than women. I can't help it, she says. "I just like that gender." That's just how she put it too. "That Gender." I just hope more men start showing up. Soon.

My mother's favorite man growing up and beyond that was her father, my grandfather. My mother always thought he was the best person she ever knew at looking at a person once and completely sizing them up. Now my mother takes great pride in being able to do the same thing, in looking at a person just once and sizing them up. She knows right away what table she wants to sit at and at what table she doesn't want to sit at, whom she wants to sit with and whom she does not want to sit with. She says she sized one guy up right away. "He's a big shlub," my mother told me. "And very boring," she added. "And they keep putting me next to him." She said every time she comes down to dinner they put her at a different table. Ever since Charlotte brought those two strange friends. "I don't even talk to her anymore," she says. "I say hello and that's it. We have nothing in common. Absolutely nothing. We're complete opposites. "She has no personality," I add. "None," my mother agrees. "No personality," she repeats. It's true. Even with her Dementia, my mother probably has the most personality here. Sometimes my mother reminds me of an aged beauty on the Titanic flitting from table to table in the ship's dining room, looking for one last glimmer of romance just before—of course—the ship sinks.

"George Clooney's Left Ear"

My mother has a poster of George Clooney on the front door of her new apartment. At her old apartment it took up the entire front of the refrigerator. Screw everyone else. There went pictures of me, her nephews and nieces and her boyfriend, my father, a post card of Marilyn Monroe, appointment cards from her cardiologist and opthamologist and hair salon and even a photo of a very fat woman to remind her and my father when he was still alive of course not to over eat. One day, out of defiance, I stuck on an article from *The Brooklyn Eagle* about me and my senior citizen readings right over George Clooney's left ear. There! Take that George Clooney! And now the photo hangs on the door of her new apartment. Not on the outside but on the inside. Later, my mother meets a woman who knew George Clooney as a kid. She invites the woman in for a chat. They talk for a long time but I don't know what the outcome is. Perhaps she never came in at all but my mother imagined she had. I'll have to make inquiries.

My mother missed dinner tonight. To be more accurate she missed the dining room. She had actually made reservations at a table down there, took an afternoon nap and over slept. By the time she got down there the dining room would be closing soon. She lost her reservation of course but they were nice enough to let her sit at one of those small tables just outside the dining room. You go day by day with my mother. Some days are good. Some days are not so good.

"There's Something I Wanted To Tell You But I Can't Think of it Now"

Tonight, for example, she sounded, for lack of a better expression, fed up. She does not like the room or the building she is living in. She does not like taking the elevator by herself. She does not like watching TV anymore. She wants to give the TV to my brother who doesn't want it. He thinks the screen is too small. "Just give it to him," she says. "I don't want it anymore." "You used to watch TV all the time," I say to her knowing full well this is no longer "used to." She's lost interest in watching TV she says. In fact, she's lost interest in pretty much everything these days. She knows she'll be there until she dies, she says with absolute conviction and resignation and at the same time not really believing it. She goes right to bed as soon as she comes upstairs from dinner. She used to be up all night. But nothing is the way it used to be. She says she hates going back to her building and apartment by herself. She wants out of that building. She gets nervous going into the elevator. Sometimes it goes past her floor. I think she has trouble reading the numbers and keeps pressing the wrong number. She is her own worst enemy. Her eyes, suffering from macula degeneration, continue to betray her. She doesn't call anyone because she cannot make out the numbers. At the end of every conversation with her, she says there is something she wanted to tell me but can't think of it. I tell her if she thinks of it she can always tell me next time. But the next time she tells me the same thing at the end of our conversation so I am convinced it is those very words themselves, "There was something I wanted to tell you" which she wants to tell me and which she always does tell me. Perhaps these words are the very bridge that connects her to me now, which connects the both of us. They are words that speak of our past and future and perhaps what lies behind them can never again be spoken but only imagined.

Tonight my mother wanted to know why they have to keep giving her all this medication. Pill after pill after pill. Spoon after spoon after spoon. I think she means the apple sauce they give her to cut the taste of the drugs 7 8 9 times a day. They find her everywhere. In the room, in the hallway under the table. This has to stop already, she says. "Look," she says. "There's a lot of things that get on my nerves here but I'm not going to complain. I don't want to make you feel upset or your wife to think I'm a bad mother so I won't complain." What she doesn't seem to realize is that this counts as complaining and is still making me feel bad. But it doesn't make me feel angry. That indirect complaining somehow makes me shake my head more than it gets me angry. My mother has clenched her fists and dug in her heels. She has rolled herself into a tight little ball like Frank Sinatra or Sylvia Plath. My mother should listen to Frank Sinatra and read Sylvia Plath. That's Life The Bell Jar Strangers in the Night Daddy Lady Lazarus. She is in for the duration. She does not want to get into that elevator at night. It's not the elevator, she says. It's her. It's not the place. "Don't get me wrong. It's not the place," she says. "It's me. It's not the food. It's me. It's not the people," she says. "It's me." Then there's a pause and she says, "But there was something else I wanted to tell you, but I can't think of it now." "Okay," I tell her. "You'll think of it next time."

"What Irish Guy?"

My mother is beginning to remember what it is she meant to say to me. There seems to be a lot. I called her rather late last night but she said she was not sleeping, just lying in bed freezing. This might be psychological or the thermostat is way down. She was angry at Charlotte again and I tried to tell her to give her some slack since she's very confused since she's suffering from Dementia. My mother had trouble understanding me and I found myself in one of those strange worlds again trying to get someone with Dementia to be sympathetic to someone else with Dementia. That might not be possible. So I drop it. I let it go. It's pointless. She said she had an appointment to meet Charlotte and another couple at a particular table in the dining room at 6. When she got there, according to my mother, the table was empty. "How could it be empty? She said." How could they not show up and not tell me? That's not right. This scared me. This can't be right, I thought." I was afraid to ask whether the other tables were empty as well. Whether she got there too early or late. I found myself humoring my mother. I entered her world. I suspended my disbelief and decided to respond to situations not only outside my mother's world but inside it as well. In other words, to humor her. She talked about meeting an Irish man at another table and having a long conversation with him. He was staying with his daughter for a couple of weeks. She couldn't understand that and I couldn't either. Where? There? Her house? His apartment? He seemed, according to my mother, very taken with her. She'd have to keep her eye on him. She likes Irish men. My mother seemed very tired. She was slurring her words again. I say this because I thought she said something about "having sex" although I could be wrong. Then again today she barely remembered him. "Who? She asked. "The Irish guy," I said. "Who? She asked. "The Irish guy,"I said. "What Irish guy?" and so on and so forth until she said, "Oh I don't know. I didn't see him."

"I'll Try Because I Don't Want to Hurt You"

Tonight my mother says there is someone in the administration who told her she was moving soon and had to get ready. This of course turned out not to be true. Another hallucination? A miscommunication, perhaps? "In case you don't know," my brother texts me, "you just spoke to her." It seems even my brother is picking up the subtle nuances of her Dementia. She told me she tried to call my brother but kept getting a busy signal. It's far more likely for my brother to get a busy signal than my mother. Busy signals and my brother are, for the most part, mutually exclusive. I told my mother she probably dialed the wrong number. She admitted the possibility. I asked if she could see the numbers. She says sometimes yes, sometimes no. She went off to find her address book. At first there was silence and then I heard her start to cry. It got louder and louder the closer she got to the phone. Oh, no, I thought. Not again. Her crying always makes me feel guilty, always makes me feel everything is my fault when it may very well be the other way around. Julie reminds me it's all part of the Dementia. To me it's just my mother crying. "I just hate my life so much, Mitchell," she says to me when she gets back on the phone. I start to fidget, to look for ways to escape the conversation. "I'm trying, Mitchell," she continues. "I'm trying so hard, Mitchell. I just want you to know that. I want you to know how hard I try. I don't want anyone telling you differently," she says. Who would that be? I wonder. Who is she blaming for spreading rumors about herself that she is not trying hard enough? My wife? Charlotte? Joanie? All of the above? "I'm walking around all day," she says, "trying to make friends but nothing. There's no one." Suddenly, and this has been happening more and more, I feel as if I'm the parent now, my mother's father not her son, ready to abandon her as her own father did her own family when he left home, when he disowned his own sons and even her after a while, the only person he ever really loved in his whole life because he felt she had abandoned him by marrying my father. My mother's deep past is a story of bitterness and abandonment and now at the age of 91 she probably feels it happening again. She wants to go back to her home. "But your home no longer exists," I tell her. "You can't go home again. Where you are now is your home and you have to get used to it." "I'll try," she tells me. "I'll try because I don't want to hurt you," she says. I try to reassure her that once we move her into the main building she'll have a better chance of meeting friends. I'm not sure myself why that's true; in fact, I'm not so sure it's true at all, but I try to make her believe it. Really, I don't think she really wants to try anymore. This is sad. This is all so sad.

"Up In the Air"

Tonight is the night she thinks I'm flying in from New York. There's a storm raging outside and there I am, my mother imagines, stuck in the skies over Florida. She panics and leaves the dining room to go upstairs and wait for my call. It reminds me of a month or so earlier, the night I flew in from New York, the night before the day she was moving when I had been delayed over an hour and she was running from neighbor to neighbor panicking, certain the plane had crashed or I had been killed on my way from the airport, imploring her neighbors to put on the news, to see if any such accidents had been reported, this despite the fact I had called earlier to tell her I had been delayed and would be there as soon as I could. But her sense of time was already beginning to leave her, so that the passing of one hour would often, in her mind, become three hours. When I call her at my usual time, she says I took 15 years off her life waiting for my call. How long does she expect to live anyway?

Ten minutes before landing, I begin to get heart palpitations. Will I die before getting off this plane, I wonder. Does my mother know something I don't? Will she now, panicking in the hallway, learn I am dead? Dead before she is? Will this finally vindicate her, justify her wild irrational premonitions of death and disaster? Or is it my premonitions of death and disaster that are giving me these palpitations in the first place? I get off the plane. Joanie's husband Cliff picks me up and we drive to the facility, my heart palpitating the whole way. The moment I get through the automatic doors there she is at the end of the hallway waiting for me. She doesn't look happy to see me. "Why are you so late?" she cries out. "I'm not late, I'm early," I tell her. "Since last night," she says, "I've been thinking about you up in the air wondering why you haven't come down already." "I'm down now," I tell her. "Yes," she agrees, "but you're going home already. "Not till Sunday," I say. "It's only Thursday." Later, on our way to dinner, she grabs my face and says, "I miss you so much. I miss you so much." Then we meet one of the nurses who grabs her to give her a sleeping pill. She tells me that my mother has been coming down to the lobby at 4 A.M. or else wandering the hallway and ending up in different residences. "Do you mean people's apartments?" I ask. She nods her head yes.

When we come into her room, she is sitting on the couch in the dark. She tells us she's been sitting there since 6:30 just thinking about a lot of things and she's made a decision. "Uh oh," says Joanie. I clench my teeth and wait for the jolt. "I don't want to stay here anymore," she says. "I'm so lonely I can't stand it here anymore," she says. "I've lived too long. Why do I have to live so long?" she asks us.

"Trouble on the Line"

It seems one of the big Dementia patient excuses seem to be about the phone. They never answer the phone. There is trouble on the line. The phone isn't working.

I go downstairs to speak to the head nurse about possibly dropping that last sleeping pill at 8 P.M. so my mother doesn't fall asleep at 8:30 and get up at 4 and so drift off into other residences or down into the lobby unkempt, unwashed and confused. I tell her I'll call her about 8:30 to remind her to go down to breakfast

"Something is Very Wrong"

I call her at 8:30 like I said I would but there's just hysteria in her voice. "What happened?" she asks. "Is there something wrong?" she asks. "No," I say. "Everything is fine. I told you I'd call at 8:30." "No," she says. "Something is very wrong. Where are you? I want you here right now. Mitchell, come here right now. I want you here immediately. Something happened." "Nothing happened," I tell her. "I told you I'd call at 8:30 and it's 8:30," I say forgetting she has lost her sense of time. "No, something happened," she insists. "Was it the car? What happened to the car?" I tell her everything is all right, to calm down, nothing happened, that I called to remind her to go down to breakfast. And as I tell her I am calling to remind her to go down to breakfast I realize how futile, how absurd it I that it is I now acting absurd not her, me trying not only to make sense out of her world but for her to make sense of a world which makes no sense—a world in which she lives far less of the time now.

"A Strange Thing Happened
To Me Last Night"

Two mornings, two tantrums. I'm in the process of taking a deep breath. For now anyway. The rest of the day seems pretty docile. My mother really likes her new room. It's bright with a big window. It's right in the center of things. You can see Charlotte anytime you want playing Bingo right next door. My mother seems much happier now but she still won't take showers or change her clothes. That problem still seems a bit up in the air. I also have to get someone to do her laundry every week or so.

My worst nightmare is her having her worst nightmare.

"A strange thing happened to me last night," she tells me over the phone. "About one or two in the morning I woke up screaming your name. Mitchell! Mitchell! Where are you!" I screamed. I went out into the hallway looking for you and screaming your name. It must have been a nightmare," she says. "Oh, God," I say to her thinking that any day now they might kick her out of this place for just such a nightmare or series of nightmares. She has been moved into the middle of things now and there is little room for error.

"Look, Let Me Talk"

Today my mother met a woman in the elevator (her new elevator) who poked her and said, "I'm going to be shampooing your hair." My mother didn't like that very much. "I don't need anyone coming in here and shampooing my hair. I don't need anyone to give me showers. Just leave me alone. Just let me live my own life," she says. "Joanie is always telling me I don't shower, that there's shit on my clothes. It's humiliating. I feel like dirt. The other day I was walking in the lobby and I heard a woman say, 'What a stunner!' She didn't say she smells. She said, 'What a stunner.' Then she asks me, "Was there anything else I wanted to tell you? " "I doubt it," I tell her. "I think you told me everything." "All the news that's fit to print." "Right," I said. That New York Times motto used to be the end of our conversations but not this time. "Look, let me talk," she says. "I don't talk to anyone all day the least I could do is talk to my son." Does she detect I want to get off the phone after just a few minutes? Whenever she says she's in deep thought it worries me terribly. She's angry at Joanie because she thinks she's stopping her husband Cliff from calling her or taking her out to dinner. She says someone was telling her that "her friend" had fainted near the elevator. She went and banged on Charlotte's door but she was all right. The man who seats her for dinner hates her, she says, and seats her with morons. She's getting more and more paranoid it seems.

"My Own Private Soviet Union"

I've hired Karen, a private nurse to help my mother. For now it's three days a week. She likes Karen. I do too but I know she needs money and would like more hours. Why wouldn't she? My mother says she's very sweet but she needs her "like a hole in the head." Well, she does kind of have a hole in her head already, doesn't she? I mean she might not need one but in a way, figuratively perhaps, she has one that can only get bigger and this other "hole in the head" I'm hiring might slow that down a little. My mother and I were talking about what day of the week it was and she said, which was a good sign because it recognized a bad sign, "Who remembers? I have a head like a sieve."

Cliff really did take her out to dinner and you might even say, a show. Trust but verify; my mother has become my own private Soviet Union. She says, they waited too long at this Chinese restaurant so they went for Pizza instead. Later they went back to her residence and they both went next door to listen to music. Cliff's version is the following: they did go out to dinner but had to wait too long at the Pizza place not the Chinese restaurant and ended up at a diner. They did, on Cliff's insistence or she'd never go, go in and listen to music. During the concert, my mother was so happy she was on a date with a young, married man, she leaned over and kissed him on the cheek, apparently more than once which prompted a woman behind them to ask "them" to stop because she couldn't see the stage.

Joanie told me to take a night off once in a while from calling my mother. I wasn't going to call tonight until I saw an e-mail from my brother telling me that my mother is wondering why I haven't called yet so I give in and call her and she sounds pretty good and tells me that Karen came by yesterday, a day she wasn't supposed to work and told my mother she must be there to help her. If this is true, we've got a problem, due to, as my mother calls it, her magnetic effect on people.

"Happy Thanksgiving"

Today my mother seems rather upbeat in a fatalistic sort of way. I couldn't ask for anything more. She needs to sign up if she wants to participate in Thanksgiving dinner tomorrow. "Whatever they have, they have," she says. Then she says, "Mitchell, I don't want you to worry about a thing. Your mother is still here. And I just want you to relax and have a good time tomorrow and the next day and the next day after that and to know that I love you." I know she likes visitors—even being interviewed by social workers. As long as no one is scrubbing her behind in the shower she can feel special. Which at least for today is the opposite of complete humiliation. Happy Thanksgiving, mom.

But on Thanksgiving Day she tells me the place is deserted. Everyone must have left to be with their families. When she went down to the dining room, she says, it was closed. The cupboard was bare. And so was hers. "So I'll wait for breakfast tomorrow," she says. So on Thanksgiving night, my mother goes hungry. Whatever it is, it is. Fatalistic. Happy Thanksgiving, mom.

"I Know What I Have to Know"

I called early today. My mother wants to switch doctors, The one thing Charlotte's mother (she means Charlotte's daughter) was smart about was dropping this guy Sherwood a long time ago. "All he wants to do is give me mental tests. What time is it? What day is it? What's your name? What Where are we? Is he crazy? I'm 91 years old. I know what I have to know. He wants to give me all these mental tests. Fine. If he wants to give them, fine. Let him take them. I'm not. "

Things are getting much better in this place, she tells me. She even went to the beauty parlor. "I was walking by the place" she tells me and they all came out and told me to come in and have my hair done. And so I did. I'm starting to meet more people too." Then Karen calls me to tell me that my mother refuses to go back to her doctor.

"Doing Everything I Can"

Who is this guy who has it out for my mother at the dining room and keeps sitting her with morons? Does he even exist?

Last night my mother called—no doubt Karen dialed—and asked if I were angry or upset with her because I sounded upset on the phone last night, as opposed to the night before when we were talking and laughing together. She says she never wants me to be upset with her because she loves me very much no matter what anybody says and that I am her whole world now. "I am doing everything here I can do really," she tells me. "Everything I can." She kept repeating this and did not ever want me to be annoyed with her. It was sad. This made me very sad.

"First Fall"

Today I received a call from Karen that my mother fell coming out of the dining room. She hit her head but it wasn't bleeding or anything just seemed a little swollen and she could walk on her own. However, they were going to take her to the hospital for precautionary reasons, meaning they don't want a lawsuit. Karen was not allowed to go with them but she would keep in touch with the hospital and let me know what happens. Later, Karen called me back to tell me they were releasing her. Thank goodness she did not have to stay overnight for I believe she may have never come back. I called the hospital and talked to the attendant nurse who told me they took x rays and her brain was normal. One can really stretch the definition of normal down here not to mention brain. It reminds me of the Henny Youngman joke about the guy who fell on his head and when they took x rays of his head they found nothing. As for my mother, I think of Winston Churchill saying about the second world war, "This may not be the end. This may not even be the beginning of the end, but it is definitely the end of the beginning." With my mother it just might be the beginning of the end.

Tonight, Karen will stay with her just in case.

And yes it may be time to look into assisted living. Assisted living? Oh God, isn't living hard enough? Or better yet isn't having already lived enough?

It's not quite death but it's certainly something like post life when you're still alive but feel you should be dead already. Sometimes my mother will break down right on the phone and cry, "Why is it taking so long for me to die? That's always the time I'll ask her things like "Did you go to any activities today?"

She's holding on for dear life. She'll never admit anything is her fault. She doesn't want to talk about it or say anything as if she blames the place for making her fall. First I thought she was going to accuse the guy, who seats her every night with morons, of pushing her. This is not over—beginning of end—this fall—her fall—the next fall. They have their eye on her.

"But To Be That Crazy?"

My mother tells me that a woman at her table told a strange story about another woman pushing her way into her apartment, pulling her pants down and saying, "I'm going to shit all over the place." "Why do they let these crazy people in here?" she wants to know. "Don't they screen them?" Well, I guess after a while people start to lose it more and more, I tell her. "But to be that crazy?" she asks me in disbelief and I start to wonder if somewhere in her mind she's worried not so much about someone like that coming into her apartment as much as she, my mother, going into someone else's place and doing something like that.

"Nine Men"

Tonight is the first time in a while my mother isn't panicking because I haven't called her yet. When I do call her, she tells me another strange dining room story. This one is about her. Apparently, they stopped her from having lunch yesterday because they claimed I told them to take her off the list. That can't possibly be true. She also complained again how they keep seating her with morons and that she's really going to have it out with that guy who keeps doing it. Maybe she's right. Maybe there is some guy who has it out for her who sits her every night with "morons," who crosses her off the lunch list and finally, tries to murder her by pushing her, not down the stairs, but more like up the stairs. Then again, maybe not.

The dining room stories have taken a sudden but positive turn. It seems my mother's Dementia is starting to work in our favor, bringing out, though in heightened form, those qualities that have made her who she is; in other words, my good old vain and narcissistic mother. The mother we have known and loved. Last night my mother had no complaints about where she sat in the dining room, but on the contrary told me how she goes down every morning about 7:30 and sits with about six men for breakfast and has a grand old time. "No, really," she says anticipating my disbelief. "That's great," I tell her. "You know," she says in case I don't know it, "I just love men. What can I tell you? I've just always gotten along better with men than women." This is great news, I tell her. Whether it's true or in her mind, it's still great news. When I tell Joanie, she laughs and says, "She told me it was nine men."

"Really? Nine?" I ask disappointed. "That means it's dwindling. The next time I speak to her it might be three, then two, then we're right back to where we started sitting with "a bunch of morons." We laugh. "Oh, well, that's Dementia," Joanie reminds me in a bubble bursting sort of way. "Last week," Joanie tells me, "she told me she sat at a table with people who went to high school with you." "With me?" I asked. "Yes, 'who Mitchell went to high school with,' she said. "I doubt," Joanie laughed, "anyone you went to high school with is living at "The Reserve." "Then again," I said, "It's possible." "Maybe one or two," Joanie said, "but a whole table of them?" "I see what you mean," I said. And despite the sadness of it all, we had to laugh.

"The 'You're Upsetting Me' Card"

Today was a good day. My mother wishes she could end it, just do herself in but she doesn't have "the guts." Later, she says not to take what she says to heart. That is not to let what she says upset me. So far there's been the mantra, "When I come down there . . ." You know figure things out, get things done. How I'm ever going to figure out this table situation in the dining room, I have no idea. My mother is depending on me but I have no ideas.

Last night was not a fun conversation. My mother made me think and feel a lot of unpleasant thoughts. I was forced to use my "you're upsetting me" card shouting her nonsensical "I want to go home" routine down. She quickly backed down and told me to ignore what she just said. How depressed she is all the time, how she fantasizes about escaping and how someone has poisoned my brother's mind against her coming back to N.Y. to stay with her. That was me, by the way, and rather than use the word poison, I'd rather say enlighten. I told her I really couldn't ignore all that. I don't believe at this point my mother can make any lasting—so to speak— friendships in this place or anywhere else at this point which certainly makes things difficult. I don't blame her for feeling how she does but I've got to do what I've got to do.

The next day there's not a peep about going home or leaving just that she has so much on her mind she couldn't begin to tell me. I'm thinking that can't be very good just on experience alone. I remember years ago when my mother's thoughts grew in her head over night like mushrooms—some quite poisonous—she'd say things like "I was up all night thinking about . . . " Or I've been giving blank a lot of thought . . ."

This would usually mean a complete reversal on something that surprised me in the first place like the time my mother thought it a good idea I move out on my own.

"Riot in the Hallway"

My mother asked me today if it would be all right if Karen could come in tomorrow morning for a couple of hours—she's feeling a bit insecure, a bit woozy in the morning. Karen helps her with the shower, puts on her make-up, does up her hair, generally makes her feel better about herself.

Today, my mother seemed in a better mood. She doesn't want to put me in a bad mood. She wishes she could get more hours from Karen. Karen makes her look beautiful. She helps her get started in the morning. She makes her feel good about herself. She went to the beauty parlor today and looked so beautiful, she says, she nearly caused a riot when she came out. "Don't look too bad for an old broad," she says proudly. Today, she says, she finally met a woman who's the same type and maybe she could hang out with her. The woman, she says, is a poet and has been to the White House. I think it was Clinton. She told her stories about Obama. She's going to the show and hopes she runs into her. I just hope she doesn't get the runs. How nice both things would be.

"Love at the Dementia Hotel"

My mother did go to the show last night. It was a singer. There was no mention of the woman she met earlier that day. Today she talked again about how Karen makes her look like a movie star. Absolutely beautiful. People stop her in the hallway. They haven't seen anyone like her in years.

My mother does seem in a better mood these days. Between Karen—who calls her every evening at about 6:30 and these men who hit on her. One such guy, Elliot, came over to her table this morning, and according to my mother, told her he's been noticing her coming and going (do either of them really know whether they are or not anymore?) and is in love with her. Well, that could be, she told him. That would definitely make sense. Later, she says, he came to her door and asked her if she wanted to join him and his son for dinner. My mother, never wanting to rush into things, told him she'd meet him for breakfast tomorrow morning.

My mother, at last, has found peace. No, she has not gone yet to meet St. Peter at the Pearly Gates, but she has gone to meet Elliot for breakfast. Apparently, they're dating. "We're not getting married," she tells me. We just enjoy each other's company. I mean, hunh? Isn't this a little fast? I mean the question I can't help asking is whether or not this is really just the other side of Dementia. I mean perhaps exaggerated joy as opposed to exaggerated depression or hopelessness? Inappropriate joy, perhaps? I mean do I really need, "Don't worry, I'll call you if I get pregnant jokes," from my 91 year old mother? Maybe her meds have kicked in. She wasn't even complaining about the dining room anymore. Apparently, her archenemy himself waited on her the other night to make sure everything was all right. I didn't say anything. The whole time she's been down there—a little over three months— I've left maybe one or two messages about something or other but never about the dining room, the infamous dining room of The Reserve where, by the way, according to my mother, the food isn't nearly as good as it used to be. But my mother is okay, kind of, about that too. And least, for now, she's not angry about it. When I told her to pass around a petition to change cooks, she just said, "We'll see what happens," like she's willing to give it time, that somehow she is acknowledging the existence of time and space and the possibility of change and that she herself could be the arbiter of change or is it that she wanted to keep talking about Elliot? At least she doesn't say the only damn thing I liked about this place was the food and now that sucks too just like everything else in my life. At least she's not saying that. For now. Like General Custer must have said to his men, "Hey, it's too quiet out there."

So I spoke to Elliot. My mother's "little friend." That used to be Karen. How did Karen turn into Elliot and if necessary can Elliot turn back into Karen again? Why not have both of them? Is that possible? Do I dare imagine such a possibility? Elliot says he's sitting next to a lovely young lady. A lot went through my mind just then. For example, is this my mother he's talking about, the same woman who's been trying to cope with a chronic unpredictable scourge of diarrhea while at the same time trying to maintain her dignity in the dining room? I said that must be my mother. He says he and my mother have a lot to talk about. Is this love among the demented? Dementia hopping at the Dementia hotel? And what if it were? I just hope he's not just leading her on. But on where? I just hope he's not after her money. What money? I just hope he doesn't break her heart. Consider she's overdue for a new pacemaker, that can't be a good thing. Hey, I think. This actually might be the real thing.

She seemed anxious to get me off the phone tonight. So now I'm being replaced by Elliot? How many times have I been replaced, ignored, humiliated, spindled, folded, mutilated by this Goddess of Vanity. Who's counting and who cares? This could be a Godsend. A mother at peace. But would God ever send a man named Elliot? Why not? A God with a Jewish sense of humor would.

"I don't want my son to think his mother's at it again," my mother tells Julie over the phone. Where did that come from? I wonder until I realize how she still thinks she's Marilyn Monroe. Well tomorrow I'll find out for myself.

Cubist Eyebrows

No, it's true Elliot is a pretty nice guy.

My mother sees a guy at the next table she told me she was hitting on before Elliot who would be very jealous if he knew. We talk to a woman in a wheelchair whose telling me how bad the weather is in New York where I've just come from. When we finally get a table she tells me how the woman is always pushing herself on Elliot who can't stand her. There's a lot of things going on here my mother tells me. I notice she's screwed up her makeup again like one eyebrow going one way and another kind of coming out of that one going in another direction. It's not just my mother with the eyebrows. I look around the dining room and notice a whole bunch of eyebrows growing out of other eyebrows, moving in all different directions. The dining room looks like a Picasso collection of cubist eyebrows.

"My Mother Used To Make Lipton Onions"

My mother is right about one thing. The food here is rather lousy. And what's with the service? How do you forget napkins? How do you bring two forks and no spoons? How do you bring someone at the table dessert when no one else is finished with their dinner? How do you serve dessert with your finger in the chocolate pudding?

Tonight, while waiting on line to be seated for dinner, a not very old man comes over to tell us how it's true some people hate the food here but that we have to remember they also hate the place and even their lives. The food, he says, is "very unusual." That's why some people hate it. They don't like change. "We have a gourmet chef here," he says, "who cooks a different kind of chicken than what their mother used to cook." Then he asks me what I'm having. I tell him the Eggplant Parmagiana. "That's an excellent choice," he says. "Well, bon appetite," he says to us and walks away. My mother says, "I'll give him a bon appetite in a minute." "A lot of crazies here," my mother says, "and he's not even that old." As usual my mother has a very good understanding of other people who are crazy and as usual very little patience for them. Funny how normal he sounded to me when I thought he might actually work here as opposed to how crazy he really sounded in retrospect when I find out he's just a resident here.

The next night he comes over again. "You know who really hates the food?" he asks me. I want to say yes, my mother and me for starters but it's really a rhetorical question. "It's the men," he tells me, "the men who are used to their mothers' plain food with Lipton onions." He smiles at me like I might remember, dare to remember you might say, my mother making me Lipton onions. I look at my mother but she's looking at me like do you see? Do you see that I'm not crazy when I talk about some of the people here? "My mother used to make Lipton onions, I tell them," he says to me. "Well, your mother's not cooking here, I say." Then he laughs and walks away.

"Where's Elliot?"

This morning, I'm worried Elliot might be dead. Just her luck, I thought. I didn't want to think that way but I couldn't help it. At this point I'm thinking, you know, to make sure things ran smoothly, that whoever had to die had to die and whoever had to live had to live. The funny thing is my mother wasn't worried at all which was worrisome. She was just curious why he hadn't called or stopped by this morning like he usually did. I texted Karen to look for him whenever she got the chance and also asked one of the nurses who "pounds" my mother with pills, to let him know if she saw him that we were looking for him. Later, during lunch, he stopped by our table. He had gone to Walmart with his family.

"Happy Hour"

Now I'm here visiting my mother and we're sitting in the "Great Room" waiting for happy hour to begin We're a half hour early so we don't have to be happy yet. But I think we are anyway. We just had lunch with Elliot and then he went off with his family who are visiting from up North and dragging the poor guy everywhere they go. He told me about his life from the time he was seventeen and joined the army during WWII—all his friends were headed to the Battle of the Bulge but he was sent to Kentucky instead to study engineering—until the time he came to the Reserve about a year ago.

When we enter the "Great Room," Bing Crosby is playing on the radio, a large 1930's or 40's radio that reminds me of the *Twilight Zone* where the man in the old age home desperately wanting to go back to his youth, finds an old radio (that looks like this one) in the basement which plays only 30's and 40's music, only the music of his youth, which only he can hear, which plays only for him. Now I feel too somehow, listening to this radio, listening to Bing Crosby, that I have been transported to another time, but not my time, their time, as if in some twisted, ironic dream I have not become young again, but old, like the people, including my mother, who surround me. I look for a way out but every exit, every means of escape, is blocked by walkers and wheel chairs and outstretched, stiffened limbs, limbs that once outstretched and stiffened like that, take time to unstretch and unstiffen themselves again.

People stare at me mostly out of curiosity but some cannot take their eyes off me. Why? I feel caught by two worlds, between past and future. The present is murky, uncertain. No, in this room now in what seems like the present is only past and future. These people in a blink of an eye, really such a short time ago, were my age and in just such a blink of an eye, and in just as short a time, I will be theirs.

A young man, his head shaven, is setting up his equipment in front of the room. He apparently is the singer. My mother is getting impatient. "Why is he taking so long?" she asks. She's anxious to start her happy hour, to be happy for an hour, at least. "Maybe there's something wrong," she says. "There must be something wrong," she says with her "there must be something wrong" expression, that expression of certainty and disgust. "Relax," I tell her." "It's not even happy hour. Not for another five minutes." "Oh, five minutes?" she asks as if she is humoring me. "Oh, I see," she says. "Five minutes." Yes, it's that moment between happy and not happy in this room, this great room, where anything can happen though really not anything that great. When the residents first arrive there is a festive atmosphere, but then a certain restlessness sets in. Some people travel clear across the room to visit someone, quite a journey really, a real commitment, for the question always lingers: Will they ever return again to the safe harbor from which they ventured? When one lady returns to her seat, which to her might be equivalent to Odysseus returning to Ithaca, she finds it occupied. "I'm sitting in your seat," the lady sitting in her seat tells her. "Yes you are," the weary returned traveler agrees. "Do you want it back?" the usurper asks. "Yes, I do!" the returner shouts.

There is a general shifting around, restless muttering going on. My mother keeps asking me if I want to sit down. Suddenly, another lady, Karen's other client, appears with her walker and places herself in front of my mother. The refreshments arrive. There is that pleasant, whirring sound of the blender in the distance of drinks being mixed. Another lady, as if appearing from nowhere, and perhaps she has, turns off Bing Crosby. I notice a man in a blue polo shirt much like my own completely bent over without meaning to be and worry that I might look like that one day. Then a young girl starts walking around with a tray handing out little pastries. When she comes up to me, I find myself trying to straighten out my spine as much as possible, hoping she doesn't think I'm one of the residents. She smiles at me but I can't tell whether she just thinks I'm one of the older residents or somewhat younger visitors, although I am the only one in the room still standing. That must count for something, but I doubt it. When she starts passing around the drinks, I take one. It's much too sweet. I believe there's supposed to be some vodka in it mixed with some tropical fruit juice, but again who knows. I tell my mother, since she's on medication, as is most everyone else I assume, not to drink too much of it. Then she asks again if I'd like to sit down. "No," I tell her. "I'm fine." Finally, the singer seems ready to go. The lady sitting in front and to the side of my mother—her name is Yvette—asks if she's in her way but my mother says no. Then, while the singer is introducing himself to the audience, my mother introduces me to

Yvette. "This is my son," she says with great pride. She seems to feel very secure at the moment. She has past, present, and future locked up—at least for the moment. Her son is with her now. Karen has already been with her and made her look like a movie star and Elliot will be returning later that evening.

The singer, young and fresh looking, begins with "I've got the World on a String." Since I've been here, I've thought of people hanging by a string but not necessarily holding the world by it. As he sings, he walks among the crowd smiling and shaking hands. Once one of these women grabs his hand they are reluctant to let him go. Yvette turns around again to ask my mother if she's in her way. My mother again tells her no. Then, as if this reminds her I'm still standing, my mother tells me this time to sit. Again I tell her I'm fine, that in fact I like standing. Then I look at Yvette. She is clapping her hands to the music. Even my mother begins to snap her fingers and I find myself videoing her doing it—just focusing on her fingers because all her energy, all her life, all she is or ever wanted to be seems to be contained within those snapping fingers. Suddenly, I find myself moving my head up and down to the music and I become frightened. I am in the moment. I am actually enjoying this. For that moment I am no longer separate from what is going on in that room but a part of it. In fact, I might as well be sitting down or else doing what looks like the Frug with Esther one of the women up front who has abandoned her walker and started dancing. Yvette turns to us and smiles. "She can really dance," my mother says to her. "Yes," Yvette says. "Am I in your way?" "No, no," my mother reassures her. Then I begin to wonder as "Witchcraft" blares through the room, whether Yvette might really be in my mother's way. But no, it can't be. Not unless the singer stood immobile the whole show in the left hand corner of the stage. The girl comes around again with drinks. One woman says to her, "I've had two. I think that's enough." Suddenly, my mother starts to get up and about halfway up she says to me, "you must be tired. Sit." I tell her I'm fine and gently push her down again. At last the singer introduces his last song, "My Way," and the audience groans in disappointment that he will be leaving soon, that happy hour will end and then, somewhere along the highways or byways of one's life, Yvette suddenly gets up and begins to move towards the back of the room. Passing my mother, she says, as if she has made some final, irrevocable decision, "I know I was in your way," and my mother still smiling, says, quite emphatically, "No, you weren't in my way at all," but Yvette, absolutely certain in her conviction that she is—and has been in the way the whole time begins to move even more slowly towards the back. I look at her face and she seems calmer now, a little more certain perhaps, not that she hasn't been, but that she is no longer in the way—not just my mother's way—but perhaps like so many of these people here—in anyone's way.

I smile at Yvette on her way out. She has a name, a beautiful name, the same name she had as a young girl, and as a woman and as an artist and now as an old woman. I remember meeting her only hours earlier, and I think how much more her face and eyes can tell me now than her words can. "Sorry if I was in your way," she says to us one more time on our way out.

My mother smiles. Even my mother recognizes she has said this one too many times. "No, problem," I tell Yvette as if perhaps she was in my way after all. Perhaps it makes her feel good, not necessarily that she was in our way because she is still able to get out of our way and thus can still make a difference in people's lives.

Then, before we even leave "The Great Room," someone has put Bing Crosby back on the radio. Or have they, I wonder, as I step with uncertainty out of one hour and into the next.

"Blood on My Vagina"

So my stress is on hold. My mother and Elliot got haircuts together. My mother wants and needs Karen so much she's willing to give up something else instead. But what? Could I be stressed about not being stressed? Could the anticipation—you know like the future that can never end well—be giving me more stress?

Most likely it's money.

It's getting a lot harder to write this since my mother's been happy. However, at the same time I am becoming more resigned to the idea that despite her recent success, her recent rally from being unkempt and depressed to the most beautiful woman in the place, there remains a certain inevitability, a physical and mental inevitability that cannot be denied—her stomach problems for one and then suddenly telling me without hesitation, rather matter of factly, that she had "blood on her Vagina" as if she had been discussing her Vagina with me her whole life. Even, or especially with, the onset of her Dementia, did I suddenly grow up in her eyes? Was I really ready, responsible enough now to hear that word? That raw, primeval, powerful word that even more than my bar mitzvah made me feel that at least, at least in her eyes, that I was at last a man? A man who was now given, who felt the right not only to make decisions regarding his mother's finances and hygiene and medication and dining room arrangements but regarding her Vagina as well? Yes, I always suspected my mother had one, but I never heard her use that word before, not in reference to herself nor to anyone else. Was there no one now to protect me from this? No, it used to be my mother herself, but really despite the boyfriend and the occasional bouts of clarity she suffers, this is not the mother I once knew who tried to keep me in the dark as long as she could, who might mention the word Gynecologist quite freely, maybe even the word "woo woo," but never the word "Vagina." And this is no doubt part of the risks, the dangers, the consequences of taking charge. That with the responsibility of being in charge comes the consequence, the stark naked reality, unfiltered, uncensored, of my mother telling me she saw "blood on her Vagina." All I could say after hanging up the phone with her was "today I am a man" and then write about it.

"Return of the Pacemaker"

Last night everything seemed to be going well. Cliff and Joanie arrived to take my mother and Elliot to dinner. That never happened. Karen is doing her hair and suddenly my mother begins to lose focus. She feels faint. She's shaking her head and opening and closing her eyes. Her pulse is down to thirty. The paramedics come and take her away. It's her pacemaker. The inevitable, overdue battery has run down. The Cardiologist has scheduled a battery replacement for the next morning. Joanie spends most of the night at the hospital with her. The next morning it's snowing and sleeting here. I almost fall twice on the ice on my way to the subway. Right before going into the subway, my phone rings. It's just before 7 A.M. It's a nurse from the hospital asking for my permission in case my mother will need blood and they have to give her anesthesia. It was anesthesia that helped get her this way in the first place. "Well, she has to have the procedure, doesn't she?" I ask. "I mean it's kind of an emergency, isn't it?" "Yes," the nurse says. "Well then yes," I tell her, taking my chances everything will go well and she won't need the anesthesia like when I agreed to sit in the emergency row on the plane taking my chances the plane wouldn't go down and I'd have to assist passengers, big and small, out the chute.

I teach my 8 A.M. class and by the time I'm done, a little before 9, my mother is already back in her room. Her heart rate has returned to normal and by 6 P.M. she's back at The Reserve. For now.

"Second Fall"

My mother fell again today. This time she hit the right side of her face. Her eye is swollen and once again she is taken to the hospital. It's Friday afternoon and I'm teaching my last class of the day. I feel that familiar buzzing of my phone from my pants pocket. My students are writing something. When I see the message from Karen that my mother has fallen, I dismiss the class and text Karen. She says she's going with my mother to the hospital and will let me know what's going on. Later, Karen texts me that my mother has a subdural hematoma—bleeding around her brain—Later, a Dr. Gonzalez calls me and tells me that if the bleeding worsens, I would have to decide whether or not to give him permission to do a more "aggressive" treatment. I tell him I worry about the anesthesia—I seem fixated now on the anesthesia—and he tells me that would be the least of it. In other words, all sorts of things could go wrong including, no doubt, her becoming a vegetable. I hate vegetables so that is definitely not an option. He asks if I have any siblings and perhaps I should talk to them about it. When I get off the phone, I think about how long I can keep all this from the one sibling I do have and then look desperately for my mother's funeral information. She's due for another cat scan in 6 hours and that's when I have to know what to do although I already know the answer to that. It's a no—brainer, so to speak. 6 P.M. passes and no one has called. That doesn't surprise me, but I start to figure that no news is not necessarily bad news. Later, Karen calls and tells me nothing had changed which I think is good news. This way, her injury might heal by itself—no boring holes in the back of her skull and sucking out the blood, or worse yet, cracking open her head and removing the clot that way. It's hard to tell though, these days, what's really good news and what's bad news. I think it's all just news. News that delays the inevitable or speeds it up.

"Heart Broken"

The next morning, the nurse calls—just to make sure I'm up to date on where my mother is and what her immediate prognosis is. I tell her I'm quite familiar with it by now but in reality I don't have a clue what's really going on. I can't see my mother's face or the doctor's face or the nurse's face or Karen's face and so I never feel like I really know what's going on. "Good," the nurse says. "We just wanted to make sure." Then she connects me with my mother.

At first, my mother cries because she too doesn't know what's happening. I tell her I know the whole story and what a story it is and this seems to calm her down. She worries Elliot doesn't know where she is. She's probably right. Then the doctor walks in. Dr. Martinez. "A very handsome doctor is taking my pulse," my mother tells me loud enough for the doctor to hear. "He's very handsome," she tells the nurse. "My pulse must be going very fast." Thank God, I think. She has found another handsome man to focus on. Only my mother can flirt with someone with blood on her brain. She asks me to call her back in a few minutes.

When I call her back she says, "I had a very bad week." Apparently, Elliot likes to be "free and easy," she tells me. Any nice pair of legs he likes to look at twice. This takes a little time for me to process Really? Nice pair of legs? Twice? Elliot? The Reserve? She tells me that before she had fallen, Elliot had taken her aside and told her he wanted to end their relationship. She starts to cry. "No one knows this," she says. "I was heartbroken. He was everything I was looking for. I was so heartbroken," she says again, "I can't tell you." Two things strike me right away One that my mother sounds like an 18 year old girl and two that she was actually looking for someone. I think I suggested a friend, but my mother always needs to take the extra step into romance. It's hard to comprehend growing up with my family, my mother and father who had been married for over 60 years who substituted fear and desperation for love and passion and how one day my mother would be crying to me over the phone at the age of 91, her heart broken, her brain bleeding, telling me how her boyfriend broke up with her. How silly, how absurd it all seems yet at the same time I am struck by the wonder of it all, how a woman's heart can still be broken at 91 and how at the age of 88 (oh didn't I mention my mother robbed the cradle?) a man can still look at a woman's legs—more than once—can still have the gall if not the wherewithal—even if he may later forget that he ever did it—to do so, and despite my mother crying, despite—or maybe because her heart is broken—life at that moment—I think to myself—might just be miraculous after all.

The reality is my mother still lies in the hospital now. Possible congestive heart failure. Not just emotionally but biologically as well. I'm not sure when to come down again. Karen calms her. She calms me too. I feel that, like my father before me, I should be skeptical, distrustful, look for hidden agendas in people, expect betrayal or deception. Everybody is too damn good around here.

The news is good. Or is it? No change. My mother's brain is on the mend. Except for the Dementia part. She lies in bed the next couple of days. She's sore. Her head hurts. She says she's very sick. She's crying again. The doctors say she can go home.

"Something Happens To My Head"

    My mother is back home. Her brain has healed. This time. She just can't keep falling on it. Why does she fall all the time? "Something happens to my head," she says. Karen needs to stay with her now around the clock. For a few days at least. Otherwise, they won't let her out. She also needs to use a walker. That's not going to happen.

"Valentine's Day"

Elliot is back. According to Karen, he and my mother had breakfast together and he's taking her out for Valentine's Day.

My mother's fall has obviously taken a toll on her and she's been rather drowsy lately and her speech somewhat slurred. That's a bad sign after being released from the hospital with a subdural hematoma.

Karen has decided to have her sixteen year old daughter help her out with my mother on the days she needs to attend to her other patient, Yvette, yes the very same lady who thinks she's in everyone's way all the time. She will also stay with my mother all night during the weekend.

"Little Mermaids"

My mother went to the doctor today. He said she should use a walker, and she said, "I'd rather die." He told her she had a close call and could have died and she said, "But I didn't did I? I'm still here."

My mother had a good day. Went to the Cardiologist. Heart checked out okay. Then she went to Happy Hour and danced with Elliot. She didn't really remember that until Karen reminded her and then it all came back. She hadn't realized how good a dancer he was. Seems like people who were around in the 1930's and 1940's are still pretty good dancers. Their legs remember even if their minds don't. But are they all little mermaids, I wonder. Tossing away their walkers and wheelchairs to dance, feeling excruciating pain in exchange for being young again even for that single hour?

"A Drop of Memory"

"Got to watch those quiet types," I tell my mother and she couldn't agree more. She sounded sweeter, happier than I've heard her in a long time. She was happy too that Karen was there. I call her my mother's memory and quite often she's mine as well. "She tells me yes or no, whatever I need to know," my mother tells me. She's fine, I think. Maybe she's okay after all. Maybe memory is overrated, more a burden, sometimes painful, sometimes bittersweet. Whomever she left behind she doesn't miss. No, she just goes with whoever and which she knows now. She lives for the moment. At this stage maybe forgetting is a good thing and when necessary Karen or I or Elliot will drop some memory into her mind and she will remember for an instant of time what it was like to dance with Elliot during Happy Hour just two weeks to the day she fell and could very well have died which I'm sure she hardly remembers anymore except for the times she says to me, "There's something wrong with my head. I don't know. I'm not going to talk about it, but there's something wrong."

"Leftovers"

It's true though, that despite, all her rallies and comebacks, my mother doesn't sound as well as she did a couple of weeks ago, before the fall. Her pre-lapsarian state—happy and innocent—willing to obey and go along with whatever of life's leftovers—and they weren't bad leftovers considering—remained. Now, after that near fatal fall, she has changed once again and not for the better. I have to always keep in mind what Joanie always says that at this stage things don't get better but only worse.

This morning my mother was already having breakfast in the dining room by the time Karen arrived at work. She told Karen she had been waiting all day for her. Karen said I would be proud of my mother but to me it was just all part of her Dementia. Got up too early, had no fucking idea what time it was, thought several hours had gone by, and then went down to breakfast.

"The Smell of Inevitability in the Morning"

Karen sent me a text this morning while I as teaching one of my classes. "I have to tell you that your mother has had a rough morning. When I came inside her apartment, there was poop on the couch, the phone was in the refrigerator and she was sitting on the couch buck naked." The last time I spoke to her everything was fine but I'm getting used to these sudden changes. Next step: my worst fear: my mother is out in the lobby buck naked doing or saying God knows what and getting herself thrown out of the place. It all starts coming together into one horrible image in my mind: The nightmare she told me about when she was screaming my name in the hallway in the middle of the night, the woman who told her about the unexpected visitor who threatened to shit all over her house. After all, isn't that what Dementia is? That unexpected visitor in your head threatening to shit all over it?

It might be time to start looking into cheaper assisted living places down there. Certainly, things will deteriorate in exact proportion to running out of money. Does anyone here smell inevitability? Early this morning on the train going to work I tried to work out a way, a plan, to keep my mother with Karen, at the Reserve for as long as possible and no matter how I figured it, that wouldn't be much more than a year.

"Someone Died Today"

Today someone died my mother and I both knew very well but I knew I wouldn't be able to talk to her about it. Sometimes we'd talk about a person dying either I heard about or she heard about and we'd talk about them for a while. How they died, how old they were, where they were buried and who they left behind. Sometimes one of us would be shocked or surprised or sometimes we wouldn't be surprised at all. "She must have been a hundred," my mother would say or "I thought she died a long time ago," she'd say or "You're kidding! How old was she? She couldn't have been as old as I am."

We often joked about death. It was my mother who always wanted the words, "I told you I was sick," or "Whatever it is, it is," written on her tombstone and whenever she would ask how everyone was, I'd say fine and she'd say fine except for Mrs. Fine who wasn't so fine since Mrs. Fine, who had been a friend of my grandmother's and who died over 50 years ago and would—as my mother and I knew—like it was some little secret between us— never be fine again.

There was very little I really could talk to my mother about these days, the days since her fall. She was always glad to hear from me but conversation seemed to frustrate her. "Something is wrong inside my head," she'd keep telling me. My cousin Audrey, her favorite niece, had arrived from California and that made my mother very happy. They sang and danced together at Happy Hour. Karen texted me and said, "Audrey is here now, so all is well." When I called that afternoon, everyone, Karen, Audrey, Elliot, were all in my mother's room. I spoke to my mother, though briefly as usual. She was trying to explain to me why Audrey was in Florida but couldn't quite get all the words out so she defaulted to the same words she had been using recently like fine, like everything was or would be fine. She was thinking positive, she was thinking forward. "But what about Mrs. Fine," I asked her. "Who?" she asked. "Mrs. Fine," I said. "Mrs. Fine isn't feeling so good," I said. "Mrs. Fine isn't so fine." I tried to say it in all kinds of different ways but I still didn't feel she was getting it. "No," she said. "But everything is all right. Everything will be all right." And then she handed the phone to Audrey and we spoke for a few minutes like we weren't really talking to each other at all and I must have sounded worried because the whole time I didn't think my mother knew who Mrs. Fine was anymore.

I wanted to speak to my mother about this woman who died today whom we both knew very well, this woman who died early this morning whose heart just stopped they said after nearly 92 years who just this morning they found lying on the couch in her room, eyes closed, her heart stopped, lying there peacefully, at last, and they took her to the hospital where they tried to bring her back. From where? For what? Humans are such fools. It just makes you want to cry how foolish humans are when they only see death, the peace and dignity of death, as something wrong, as something to be avoided, because each miserable breath is always better than no breath at all. No, she was gone now. Gone for good and finally even those men with their meat-like hands and their death machines that tried to keep one alive for no other reason than to avoid death; even they had to admit she was gone and the next day she was put into a beautiful casket, not the most beautiful one, but certainly beautiful enough, and they explained how good it was she had reserved one 25 years ago and pointed out the difference in price, the difference between now and 25 years ago, pointed it out like a lesson in inflation, made her son look at the numbers and sign his name acknowledging he had seen that difference and appreciated it so he'd know she was in the right place where her husband waited for and how the rabbi spoke not as if he knew her, this rabbi who told the son only hours before how his own mother had been killed by a drunk driver and how he now forgave him and was sure after 13 years in prison he hopefully would straighten out his life, this man who ironically was the only one in his family, much like the son he was talking to now, who ever took care of his mother despite having so many sisters and brothers who couldn't wait till he got out of prison not because they wanted to see him free but to see him free them from the burden of taking care of their own mother, this rabbi who did not falsely speak as if he knew this woman, but only as if he had been told great things about her. And the son thought his mother might have liked him despite the fact she would not have wanted a rabbi to speak about her at all, especially who didn't know her at all but despite that he spoke of her great sense of humor which the son told him all about and of her passion for life and how in the end especially had brought joy into the lives of those she came in touch with, whom she had made laugh or dazzled with her enduring beauty, just a little better, and then was squeezed into the same lover's crypt as her husband who had been waiting patiently for a very long time, through the span of two more boyfriends, and it was things like this I would have liked to tell my mother all about because it was with my mother I enjoyed speaking to about other people and how they ended up and now I knew I would not be able to talk to her about it—anymore.

Removing George Clooney

I knew heading back to my mother's apartment would be the hardest part of all this. The most painful and gut-wrenching part of this whole ordeal of cleaning up after my mother's death, harder even then the funeral itself.

As soon as I walked into her apartment, not even 30 hours since Karen found her lying dead on her couch, I did not walk over to the couch, not right away, and imagine her lying there, eyes closed, brow finally unfurled, relieved of pain, at peace at last. I did not go over to her bed and imagine my mother lying there where she slept for the last night of her life, nor the sink whose faucets were still running when her aide found her, nor the toilet or shower or photos of earlier, happier times, of her high school graduation, of the beautiful blonde girl sprawled on the grass who my father must have looked at every day of his life in disbelief he had married this girl, that such a girl had agreed to marry him, and the one of this girl and my father, he now looking young and handsome in his army uniform and of my mother and dad years later in front of their condo not ten miles from here or her granddaughter Anna—no the first thing I looked at the moment the front door closed behind me was the poster of George Clooney still taped to the door and I imagined putting that poster, standing it up, on its own chair at her funeral service—just like at my mother's 90th birthday party—and me thanking him during my little eulogy for making my mother happy these last several months or perhaps I would slip it into her coffin along with some other photos of my mother and father or my mother and her boyfriend Harold or her latest boyfriend, Elliot—just roll up George and slip him inside her coffin with everyone else.

But I would not do either. Yes, George Clooney's poster was the first thing I looked at because it reminded me of the things I liked best about my mother, her wonderful relentless, irreverent shameless, infectious, sense of humor; her wild and crazy and infuriatingly endearing and enduring fantasy life; her feistiness and her unique kind of wisdom, not the wisdom of a saint or a philosopher perhaps, but of a woman who despite fearing life, always fearful of what it might bring, yet who at the same time tried to squeeze as much pleasure out of it that she could and when I looked at George Clooney, there was something in his eyes that seemed to know this and I thought to myself as I gently removed him from her door, perhaps the hardest thing I ever had to do, that he would definitely have liked my mother.

Mitch Levenberg was born on 9/14/52 in Brooklyn New York. He has published essays and short fiction in such journals as *The Common Review, Common Boundaries, Battle Runes, Fiction, The Saint Ann's Review, The New Delta Review, The Same, Big City Lit.com, Local Knowledge, Confluence, Fine Madness,* and others. His collection of stories, *Principles of Uncertainty and Other Constants* was published in 2006 and his collection of short essays, *Write Something,* in 2014. His short play *Hippopotamus* was performed at the Unboxed Voices short play festival in 2014. He teaches writing at St. Francis College and lives in Brooklyn with his wife, daughter, and five dogs.

Irene Weinberger Books publishes a limited number of literary works in e-book and trade paperback format, often in collaboration with other presses.

We assume a graceful style, whatever the genre and whether the tone of the work is edgy, realistic, poetic, humorous, or experimental. We look for powerful narrative momentum, whether the story is highly plotted or superficially uneventful.

Irene Weinberger Books is an imprint of Hamilton Stone Editions.

To see our catalog, go to www.ireneweinbergerbooks.com.

www.ingramcontent.com/pod-product-compliance
Lightning Source LLC
Chambersburg PA
CBHW021132130626
46554CB00002B/972